ObliviOnanisM

OBLIVIONANISM

I: *Dissolving*

M. O. N.

gnOme

So, happier than I had ever dared hope to be, I dissolved again into that native infinity of crystal oblivion from which the daemon Life had called me for one brief and desolate hour.

H. P. LOVECRAFT

CONTENTS

Indescribable

The indescribable thoughts that passed
through her mind as she spontaneously
slipped the unknown, semi-ovoid
object into her already wet anus are
understood only in the dreams of the
now slumbering divinity who crafted it.
Nothing had caused her to take it from
among a little collection of statuettes
and charms offered out of an ebony
box. Neither selected nor received, the
thing had found her warm hand without finding, through a gravity or
sympathy so weird that it has no medium, no means other than its own
instantly inevitable happening. No
hint, glint, or glistening moved her eyes
towards it. No scent or memory or
suggestion made her mouth sweeten
with saliva at the thought of touching
it. Yet they did, as if the nothing, the
eternal void, had created itself anew
and for her alone in palpable form, the
shape of the potentiality of every

pleasure, the pure *quodlibet* of perversity: whatever you want. If someone were at that moment given inner sight of her face, the depth of the image would drown all facts.

A flurry of untraceable intentions and nervous movements immediately followed this first contact. It was hers, as the gentle smile from her generous friend confirmed. But becoming hers the thing suddenly felt stolen and secretly demanded to be hidden away. 'Thank you . . . I don't know . . . Ciao.' In the moments marked by these ellipses two events occurred. One: A wave of self-consciousness about the beauty of her long dark hair swelled from solar plexus to crown and then washed in slow cascade down the subsurface of her body, softly electrifying in turn every follicle, upturning in tiny erection each pore of her pink-white skin. The sensation made her feel afresh the emptiness of her abdomen and lent her limbs a mannequin, languid air. Countering the awkward, quasi adolescent order of this hollow qualm—like finding that your body is a only misplaced puppet doll queasily tricked out with glazed eyes and glossy hair—she, whose name was Gemma, breathed two deep breaths. Their repetition re-licked the life-flame deep within her, embering her sacrum and flushing further the visibile *barzakh*, the lovely lines, between her biological and etheric bodies. Not yet lust, but the fertile ground, the vermicular soul-body debate from which all horniness weedily grows. Is my hair alive or dead? *Please, love, let yourself be buried in the tomb of my body.* Two: A psychodramatic answer to the existential mystery of embodied individuation overcame her. This took the dreamy form of an excessively cinematic lesbian fantasy positing Gemma and her blondish friend—without either have seen either film—at the supremely hot and Sapphically spliced intersection of Dario Argento's *Suspiria* and David Lynch's *Mulholland Drive*. How else could the eroto-scholastic *sic et non*, the sexy battle of the sublime brows, ever be worked out? The close co-presence of their two pairs of same-colored eyes, the courteous proximity of slightly different sized breasts, of singular belly buttons, the caressable and easily crossed gap of a small but noticeable difference in age, their perfectly shared readiness for spontaneous tribadism—all was simply too much to hold out of mind. Whence at once they share dangerous coven-secrets while treading water in the blue-tiled baroque pool of Gemma's brain, their heads of hair remaining afloat, one a little higher than the other, by neck-long curls. A nyadic double decapitation, cephalic girlfriends of Orpheus, bobbing amorously above silhouetted and rhythmically scissoring aqua-light limbs. Then, in a bedroom walled by the creepy hum of cosmic night, the pretenses of wig, couch, and towel are cast aside. Here one does succeed in waking the other, with a goodnight kiss. *Thank you, for everything.* The inescapable erotic gravity keeps falling into a nest of barbed wire from being the only window of escape. *Have you ever done this before? I don't know, have you?* Oblivion . . . .

No memory remained of her trip home, no recollection of ignoring an acquaintance near the newsstand, of holding her purse with perverse tightness, of enjoying for the first time the general fact of war. It was like she lived

4

on the other side of Lethe. Now that she had entered the object so strangely within herself in a perfectly innocent and indecent way, everything was different. Anal. Here she simply lay, hardly reclining, more like leaning into falling into sitting on the sofa, but already against the headrest, not even half-undressed, the elastic of her underwear on one leg stretched irreparably aside, pants pushed out of the way merely enough for their constriction to still shove and hold (from her own hips' bending pressure) the warming thing higher and less voluntarily into her velvet and rosy canal. Cloaca: the single end opening serving for sex and waste-evacuation in non-placental animals. Being sort of well-read, Gemma's intellect had to endure the pleasurable fast evaporation of many erudite and ridiculous thoughts. But *she*, she had already left and safely observed all from the solar perspective of the molten love upworming itself into her body's oceanic depth, causing her head to swim with happy dizziness and dreamy, febrile distraction.

Lust, the lubricious insertion of inevitable longing for the divine beyond into the matrix of the mind's evolutionary entanglement with corporeal form, became her. As the phenomenal sphere slowed to the sweetness of a placeless present, Gemma's feeling of her flesh, her essential and intimate sense of having a body, started to forever and slightly dissolve, to lovingly decay in layers no substance could properly measure and no language do more than alluringly whisper. These, the infinite invisible veils that make up the fabric of her being-in-the-world, one by one became manifest as no longer anything more than the thousand special effects that saturated and flashed within the fractal-deep surface of her skin. Warm glows wound themselves in waves around her bottom and back up (or down?) the insides of her thighs. A micro dew of pearly sweat moistened the underside of her breasts, making the bra cups creep upwards and tenderly pressure the pendant mammary pools beneath. Her exhale— O lovely dilemma of the breath's genitive!—slowly parted Gemma's lips and she started to barely sense that strangely full voidal space inside and beyond the opening of her mouth which all whores in heat feel bound to flick and tongue. The tint of her neck veins deepened, pimping her pleasure like a coral blue-green undergrowth, the exuberant swarming of a life beneath her life. A kind of anti-gravity enveloped her wrists, causing her freshly hot and tranquilized heart to flash with a reflection that at any moment her hands might without mental command be found fingering a spit-wet nipple and/or humping her sweetly swelling clit. Miniscule shocks and tremors traversed her subtly unhinging form— the typical erotic tingling. Eyelids descended by an immeasurable minimum, gracing their proportionally opening pupils with the transporting gaze of a Magdalene sanctity. She saw her own body in the sublime light of a possession beyond ownership, close to the way Ooliba looked at paintings of Chaldean warriors: not aesthetically sensing the adorable image, but already seeing and tasting each of its superlative originals, all the perfect oiled organs whose strength instantly lay only in the surrender through which they definitely will—whether in turn or simultaneously no one can tell—freely fuck all her endlessly opening holes.

Looking at nothing, everything became peripheral and paradoxically more present, like an unbounded magic fabric, all interwoven and the more together for being centerless. Every perspective was lost. Vanished the prison of foreshortening. Totally overcome was the limit of the helpless eye that almost dies to see around its own corners, to glimpse the curves and creases and moist folds about which only another's supplicant tongue can ever give accurate report. For the first time Gemma now saw her pure surface perfectly from within. Her form became a perversely sacred site where the polysemy of *the way she looked* found itself in unthinkable but wholly palpable harmony with itself, a specular place akin to the impossible visionary intersection of an intoxicated mistress and her blindfolded sperm-soaked love-slave. She saw herself. Not a secret inner self. Not an imagined self. And absolutely not the sort of girly-girl self-image that magazinely leads so many by the nose into the consumerist-capitalist maw of self-made monstrosity. Gemma saw herself as she actually appears: beautiful. She saw herself fatally so, and thus she began, finally, helplessly, to become her own demon-lover, a soul totally and intimately *possessed*, by its own body.

Gemma did nothing. Nothing happened. Nothing else could happen. Maybe nothing else ever had happened. And there was no going back. She was still dressed. How? New tight black jeans. Azure blouse, a little unbuttoned and rolled up to the elbows. Heavenly light blue bra with matching hipster panties. Goldish socks. Shoes. She enjoys it all: the neat, disciplined feeling of taught denim fashioning the young fat of her thighs, the light pull of inevitable pressure around her armpits and abdomen, the lazy way the fine gold necklace lay snaky and relaxed on her reclined bosom, the triplex contrasts of dark half-open pants overlapping upstretched underwear around a patch of hip-flesh becoming pinkly tinted and more tender by the surrounding dissartorial taughtness . . . Every line she sensed, as clearly as if she were herself the crystal mirror through which all geometries of surface, every apparent topology of her lush form, are always by myriad angelic master artisans being simultaneously and effortlessly limned. But no line mattered, none kept or touched her, circumscribed her, the beautiful untraceable one. Rather all color and line of her simple clothes, and most of all every openly secret relation between body and covering—covert diaphony being the essential substance of all style—was made by a strange interior becoming all the more beautiful and meta-elegant under the heady influence of the swiftening acceleration of her absolute indifference to them, which, outpacing aesthetics at every turn, incarnated her form with the weight of a fatally qualified proverb: clothes might make a man, but never the woman.

For half an hour Gemma lay, neither asleep nor awake, unconscious nor dreaming, here nor there, moving nor still. She had fallen into being more alive, and more dead. The story of this half hour is an untellable tale of infinitely intertwining thoughts and images, a tapestry of terrifyingly successive concepts and visions, the sum of which might be imaginatively glimpsed in the form of a four-dimensional Boschian tapestry. The space of this tapestry, as if woven by aroused androgynous elves on some five-dimensional non-Euclidean loom, comprises four axes of experience: 1) fragmentary erotic fantasies; 2) ideas for creative projects; 3) unspeakable spatio-temporal distortions; 4) words, language. If you were an eye that could roam and swim this interweaving psychic stream, vision might flash with reflections like the following:

An eight-month epistolary drama of cross-species conspiracy comes to conclusion in an aestival midnight orgy: panting on all fours in the dewy grass, Gemma feels the heat of two aristocratic satyr-cocks pull at once from her raw flesh to drench her face and back with semen suffused mid air by the first instant rays of rosy-fingered dawn . . . Someone invents a psycho-biological time-machine for same-life metempsychosis: Gemma risks life and limb to steal the contraption for the express purpose of beginning a multivolume exegetical commentary on *The Story of O* at the age of 12 . . An art

professor is driven into terminal auto-
erotic erotomania (the delusion that
one is in love with oneself) by a series
of symbolically coded neo-Balthusian
self-portraits painted by Gemma in
perfect imitation of the professor's own
style, submitted for final review with
an accompanying couplet: "Speak the
true name these gnomic images say, /
See me become your love-slave for an
endless day" . . . The little crease between Gemma's brows—true orgasmic
signum—are slowly and lovingly
opened by an occult phantasmatic
gravity into twin alpine valleys filled
with equally superior and non-violently
always-warring homosapienic cultures:
Gemma immediately incarnates there
as a shepherdess about whom romanc-
es are written on uterine vellum for
three centuries . . . A new erogenous
zone is brought into being by the acci-
dental radio-transmission of a
mathematized amateur theory of psychic self-hoaxing: capitalism is
everywhere brought to immediate end
as all consumers become occupied with
touching precisely what the commodity
can never give . . . A Dionysian boy
half-dozing on a beach in Seychelles

hallucinates Gemma swimming topless
in the surf: the noon-day nocturnal
emission draws the olfactory attention
of a million houri . . . Three anonymous poetic geniuses independently
send Gemma diurnal gifts of priceless
sex toys appended with philologically
inter-animating love lyrics: she or-
gasmo-exegetically experiences all
semantic permutations. Et cetera.

Gemma returned to so-called reality from this ecstasy only to discover a
most uncanny transformation in the
fabric of her life-world. At the level of
concepts, the transformation is express-
ible by saying that *she no longer cared*.
It was not that she became indifferent
or neutral or disinterested toward the
world and the fact of her being in it.
Indeed she was more interested, more
delighted with the possibilities of
things than she ever thought possible,
as if the relation between thought and
potentiality had suddenly bottomed out
into an unimaginably vast and magnan-
imous subterranean cavern of which
the historical world is only a pale
shadow. But the truth, the real fact of
her no longer caring was much more
than concept, in the same way that the

breath through which one lives is much more than oxygen. In fact her no longer caring, her falling into being beyond care, took as its first locus and sign a new experience of her breath, a tranquil delight in breath itself as an inexhaustible suggestion of innumerable pleasures. Rather than simply breathing, like a fish, Gemma's breath now expressed a new intelligence that could touch and penetrate the immanent radical plenitude of a self-permeating field of magnetic delight. Each breath now not only provided a dose of the aerial substance her body needed, but achieved itself as a unique and fresh drawing of a line of openness passing from the outermost edge of everything into a profoundly specific yet instantly diffusing point in her body. Every inhale was like a little drop-bubble from the Outside that entered through her face, transpired the moistest limits of her lungs, and dispersed in a tiny explosion when it found its target – a spot spontaneously but not randomly selected by the thought-desire that activated and directed it. Her no longer caring, not a withdrawal but a deepening of atten-

tion, formulated itself in direct relation
to the activity of her breath, an activity
that constituted a new synthesis of
thought, desire, and flesh. In this she
became more aquatic, more like an
animal creature saturated with the
element of its life. Thought, desire, and
flesh were inter-integrated, non-
reductively and triunely fused within
the processive marine pulse of her
being. Realizing this, Gemma began
slowly to lead her breath around her
body, sometimes incrementally displac-
ing it from where it had been,
sometimes moving it in the next moment somewhere else entirely. Where
the former movement had the effect of
fractally opening up new space within
the minimal interval marked by the
increment, expanding and stretching
open the sensitive territory available for
this subtly external self-touching, the
latter dynamically connected disparate
parts of her form into a meta-agile
membrane of affective auto-erotic
flight. Navigating her breath here and
there within her flesh, allowing spirit
to play with her body in an open-ended
way, Gemma initiated herself ever
deeper into the loop joining imagina-

tion and reality. Locating herself, feeling her way of being to be differentially more and more a current on this circuit, Gemma thus drew her body into the first step towards its becoming an occult pornographic portal, an opening of terribly delightful and intimately abyssic dimensions.

Gemma did not know this as such. She did not know what was happening. Not because she was in ignorance, but because she was herself the happening of it, and there was nothing else to know. It was a little like falling into somewhere where one already is, so that the sensation of falling, instead of being a frightening loss of ground, feels like the lightest sinking into somewhere more and more safe, as if it were possible, by a kind of erotic gravity, to let oneself effortlessly edge more extremely into place, until place itself begins to subtly erode and open towards incredible horizons of thrilling enclosure. Gaining new imaginative and sensitive entry into the grottic space of her body, Gemma started to participate in the perversely expansive and wayward parameters of self-love. Psychically surveying her form with a perfect balance of intensifying detail and harmonic synthesis, she withdrew from the idea of world-life and drew herself into the lucid depths of feminine claustrophilia. There was something hopelessly pleasurable and endlessly significant within her, a fatal opening that had always been waiting there, precisely because the place of its waiting engulfed every other place, every *where*. The only way to approach it, to have any hope of feeding it, of being swallowed by it, was to touch herself. Suddenly the way forward became clear. To truly taste the sweetness that she will become, Gemma must loosen and twist her total body in delicate straining towards her innermost, essential hole. She must self-mutate into a divine organ of the pentecostal self-burning of desire, the unquenchable flame of annihilating love, a tongue rimming the void.

Golden

A descending autumnal sun began to illuminate the treetops Gemma could see from the couch where she still lay, looking langorously through her east-facing windows out over rooftops towards the graveyard beyond. *E tu vivrai . . . L'Aldila*. Delighted by the fiery colors, she went into a reverie that made the subtle movements of her pupils fall into resonance with the mobile pattern of her breath. Seeing and breathing fell into a golden rhythm, each helping the other submit more fully and co-proportionally to the extraordinary dying solar color that the world at this moment would not stop giving her mind. The more her gaze penetrated the substantial aura of the arboreal glow, the more beautifully she breathed, the more lovely she looked. Slowly drinking in the intensity of this perceptual vibration, Gemma entered the sweet and terrible circuit of beauty perceiving beauty, becoming something thoroughly shot through with it. There was no danger of her not passing beyond, because she squeezed most intimately through, the place where it is written, *Narcissus was here*. Via the operation of a native infinite intelligence, Gemma was already deeply into the other, impossible side of the I-love-myself equation, already deflowering Narcissus's image from behind, mercifully accelerating the boy's desire-drowning from within the phantasm.

But now a new gravity made itself known. A meta-breath, a breath within and beyond her breath, was drawing the inner touch-point of her respiration ineluctably down towards the supremely familiar yet fundamentally alien object in her bottom. She had neither forgotten nor remembered it was there, but had rather only felt its presence precisely by eliding the idea that it was an object as such. What was it, and is it still now what it was? Every tiny motion had worked to confirm both its being there and its being other than what entered her. Inversely, every momentary stillness had reified at once its absence and its being exactly what

she entered herself *with*. Gemma capri-
ciously imagined that just as a gem is
something very different from the stone
of which it is made, so the ovoid thing,
under unconscious magic influence of
her name, might have somehow trans-
formed into something different, but of
the same substance, than what it was.
A ridiculous thought, she thought, in
the instant that thought occurs without
having to think about it. But also an
accurate index, she knew, of something
too real, a direct sense of and a way of
saying that the thing had changed, in
tandem with the fact that it had
changed her. Whatever she thought, all
of her thought, in dialogue with her
deepening breathing, was bending
towards it, but in a looping way such
that the more she thought of it, the
more the thing itself proved impossible
to think, the more intensely the feeling
of it fluttered back upwards towards
the brain through which her mind was
worming into the idea of what was
penetrating her.

Gemma's eyes remain fixed on the
immanent flame – a gold that looked
like it was engulfing the world. As her
thoughts encircled the idea of what was

within her body, and as her breathing
burrowed further into its own ability to
touch the secretly extended and specific places where flesh and soul
lasciviously meet, her gaze intensified
itself in helpless transfixity. She had to
gaze, she had to look the way she did.
Doing so was the only, inescapable
means of erotic transport, and her eyes
took it. By drowning, not in, but beyond the *this* that bound her vision,
Gemma's ocular reverie thus proved
itself a perfect medium between the
elsewhere look of rapture and the
focused look of desirous staring. Staring into the gold increased her desire,
but only by sending it away in a way
that made her stare all the more. She
thus sensed a weird kind of spilt or
space electrically opening up within
her self-interface. On the one hand, she
felt that she was being increasingly
absorbed by the beautiful color. On the
other hand, she felt that she was per-
petually falling away from it. From the
perspective of the concept of self, it
seemed that her mind was separating
more and more from her body. From
the perspective of the concept of world,
it seemed that her mind and body were

becoming more intimate. The secret
relation between these movements, the
term that proved them two sides of a
single becoming, was her breath,
which, in one and the same flow,
worked to dissipate and hold herself
together in an *expanding contraction*.
On the side of her self, the inside,
breath filled up the fissured space
opening between mind and body. On
the side of the world, the outside, her
breath expanded the closing space
between body and mind. Stretched
between the *exstasis* of vision and the
instasis of auto-affection, Gemma
stayed more and more within her
breath because her breath was becoming less and less hers, because
breathing deep into her nethermost
body was the only way of not drowning, of breathing *in* a blissfully marine
world.

Deciding in favor of something
that might happen, Gemma started
slowly to remove her clothes, without
breaking for a moment her gaze into the
brilliant beyond. The way she removed
them was incredible, and probably
impossible to imitate. The sequence
and pattern and style of her stripping

proceeded by a kind of alien, unrecognizable rhetoric, as if her body were taking haptic dictation from a terrifyingly intelligent and charismatic otherworldly voyeur. Artless and planless, Gemma's hands unfolded her nudity with the touch of an angelic whore, with gestures manifesting the dexterity of a being created solely as slave to its beauty. This natural, spontaneous, and wholly unrepeatable ritual of undress constituted an inside-out *blazon* that killed forever or impossibilized the future of this poetic form. Any Petrarchan sonneteer who saw it would be bound to immolate his dismembered body on a pyre of burning lyrics.

The disrobing began with her breasts, where a vague electric pulse suffused her stiffening nipples and felt the need to be released like a sparking pink current into the open air. Sensing their fatal perspectival symmetry, as if subtle thread had spiraled itself tightly around the points of her titties and was now pulling on both from an untouchable vanishing point, Gemma eased her bodyweight evenly between her ankles, supporting herself in a splayed Japanese or *seiza*-style sitting posture. The shift from side to center had a double and contradictory effect on the dense nexus of her moist groin, opening it to the airspace flowing between her legs and around the small of her back as well as constricting her cunt tighter in the underwear stretched gently across her bottom just below the top of its cleft. The movement finished pulling apart her pants zipper and left her soft cheeks more open to radiate the subtle heat travelling up from her tight thighs. The left side of her panties was still trapped in her butt cheeks, bunched in the crevice and pinched onto the ex-posed side of the probe from when she had pushed in with pure, seamless surprise. Now, as Gemma's hands met at the unbuttoning of her blouse, her tender sphincter quickly sucked harder at the egg-like intruder as if the fibres of her rear-flesh knew pulsating fear that the thing might exit. *Ravish my ass, dilate my infernal rose until I quake with bliss. The supreme spectacle of my cumming will drive every empyreal Beatrice to deliriously stroke her clit.* Gemma hardly thought that, but for sure she felt something similar as her back gently arched, lowering dark brown locks towards her behind and opening her pale neck before the colors holding her green eyes captive in the late evening light.

The innumerable portions of the world for which the possibility of being within sight of Gemma's breasts now became more desperately immanent found themselves at a loss of what to do. No one saw her. And for this reason, because no *one* saw her, everything within sight of her decayed in a sweet burning, found itself (solely by virtue of being there) saturated in the self-eroding erotic acid of almost witnessing Gemma more nude. Such was the vibrationally expanded fact, the plane of immanence radiating outward from the tiny frictions between the light blue bra fabric and the tawny-pink tips of flesh encircled in the open secrets, the perfect topologies of her areolae. The eye of the world, *oculus mundi*, was on her breasts, splitting itself into an endless many in the hope of a better look. Feeling the gravity of this infinite observation, of the twin fruits of her chest as the very remaining visible of life, Gemma wanted bad to offer them to the world. Can

you take part of your body and give it,
to everything? Were it possible she
would, placing her breasts on some
kind of supremely open auric plate for
all to taste and see how sweet she is.
Presented there, in the gift of sincere
abandon, they would like (n)ever-
consumed offerings to temple gods,
perfumely waste away in the intimate
ever-lasting expenditure of staying
untouched. Becoming forever hers by
being given without relinquishment,
they would unfinishingly unveil a
precious interior fullness in the supreme form of sublime exposure.
Opened to being beyond her body by
holding parasitically onto all that is
within it—breasts give suck by sucking
from the giver—they would simply
through uncovering feed a whole world
by gently stretching and spreading
apart its subtlest aesthetic fabrics,
peeling the seeing eyes of each thing
inside out into tender greedily tasting
mouths, as if the destiny of the pupil is
infantilely fellatial and all things were
pupil—a myriad of opening and closing
toric voids, infinite O-rings milking life
into the torturous untouchability of
their own auto-spectral space.

Such quasi-thought geometric fantasies entrusted Gemma's mind fleetingly to the self-saturating phenomenon of her pale, post-adolescent breasts, blushing her tactile imaginarium into the shape of a hot magnetic current flowing between verdant eyes and rosy nipples, like some kind of invisible light-worm: out one eye, down into the mouth, out one breast, into the other, out the mouth, into the other eye . . . Twisting and crossing through the moist intersection of her mouth, the vital spiritual hole at which the current at once entered and exited, this aetherial lavatic flow teased transparent slick saliva towards the dark pink insides of her lips, pooling the lubricant-to-be near the tip of her tongue. Inhaling her bosom higher towards the oral excitement of her transported face, as if the imperceptible unconscious sway of her tongue could easily charm the nerve-tendrils of her nipples invisibly up into her waiting orifice, Gemma instinctively gaped her mouth with enough nipple-thirst to allow a sinuous, syrupy drop of viscous drool to descend on the center of one tit and, with a tiny turn of her chin, to fall perfectly on the other –

the liquid suspended between them now cohering into a new dewey jewel that fell to her bellybutton only to repool and creep its way towards the sometimes-trimmed top of her pussy.

The instant elegance of the motion was among the first objective signs that Gemma's mind-body correlation was becoming undone and entering headlong into a dangerous spontaneity, a no-place where the distinctions between thought, feeling, and action become blissfully and vertiginously untenable. She started to intuit with new clarity the indissoluble links between the noetic content, the affective vector, and the space-time location of a thought, so that the possibility of playing and stretching her consciousness between these poles appeared more and more viable. Of course this possibility appeared, not abstractly or in general, but in the specific form of the slippery trickle of spittle that tickled onwards across her abdomen towards her clitoris. Her gaze still more deeply bound by the rich light of the lowering sun, Gemma inwardly saw the crystalline liquid with a combination of sensation and desire that insisted on

the solubility of their difference and
thus on the possibility of really direct-
ing the descent of the droplet without
having to direct it as such, that is, not
by the operation of a volitional command exercised on the vibrant liquid
matter, but by a literal and instant
agentive *feeling* of its way through the
sub-empirical pathways and psychical
sensitivities of her ripe and lucid skin.
Naturally she wanted her spit to drip
by itself through her diaphanous panties onto the top of her pussy and
suffuse the outside of its swelling lips
with the wet gloss of a virtual tasting
and tonguing. Naturally she did not
want to manually short-circuit the
process by using her hand, the tool of
tools, to merely and messily move the
saliva there. But even more naturally
did she want to happen what actually
did happen exactly by virtue of her
wanting it to, within the thought-
feeling-action dynamism of her desire.
Here there was no question and answer, no before and after, no cause and
effect. As if the force of wanting really
burst out of relationality and achieved
total creative transitivity, as if the
subject-object correlation sodomitically

suicided itself on its own phallic vector, Gemma *wanted* her slippery
wanton saliva right onto her clit, drew
it there via ducts no anatomist could
ever discern. Without a doubt, the
terrible seed of self-love embedded
within her was spreading differentially
in unpredictable, pestilential ways.
Virally, Gemma's whole body was
becoming haptic.

The hot contact between the slimy
oral syrup and her warm cunt coincid-
ed with a weird, lacy flash of light into
her eyes, as if the gold foliage of the
trees became temporarily reflective. For
a second she thought the illusion might
be the work of an ancient species of
liminal demonic spectre that uses
flashing color to temporarily suspend
the minds of their hosts. But she knew
this was not the case, knowing herself
to be totally, almost frighteningly
awake. The flash was due to something
Gemma did not guess but would come
more and more to know: the ever-
strengthening emergence of the same
power within herself, an ability to
hypnotically possess bodies, wholly or
in part, with flashes of her own beauty.
This power, though aesthetically dis-

tinct, was simply the visual projection of the becoming-manual of her own body, the actualizing potentiality of her sight to touch, extramissively as it were. Transmissable across gross, subtle, and mental forms and bodies, it could be activated by Gemma's corporeal, imaginative, or intellectual gaze, or any combination thereof. The power did not overtake all aspects of these three kinds of vision, only the part pertaining to her own good looks. It activated automatically whenever Gemma *looked* at something in any of these senses (physically, imaginatively, intellectually) with her own loveliness in mind. Her *look* (seeing, imagining, and/or thinking) in this mode operated as a self-reflection of her form that presented, like some unpredictable parabolic mirror, a dangerous glamour, an intermittent luminous excess that possessed whatever it touched via subjection to the spectacle of its own essential unpossessability. Neither rhythmic nor arhythmic, the flashing would hold its 'victim' helpless for a little longer than the look lasted, giving its being over to the strange loops and

twisted becomings of Gemma's pro-
found desire.

As the anal object was implanting
this power within her, so it seamlessly
became the first thing that Gemma
exercised the power upon. It is hard to
specify, however, how deliberately she
utilized this power, because the power
itself came as if coded according to
subtle, differential increments of delib-
eration or intentional willing-moments.
She had slipped the thing pretty deep
into her ass totally spontaneously,
without any planning to do so whatsoever. Slightly less spontaneously did
she transitively desire her saliva down
into the pink wettening flesh of her
fragrant pussy. The event was desired,
but the happening of it itself was spontaneous, without whence or wither.
The tripartite turning of her self-
reflective attention towards the neither
inert nor mobile alien form still entering her rear was slightly more
intentional. She wanted her gaze there
with more causal force than mere
wishing, but nowhere near any recognizable degree of purposefulness.
Stretched curvingly between the wan-
ing golden light filling her eyes and the

faintly sodomitical sensations beginning to perverse her anal nerves, Gemma's inordinately magnetized consciousness somehow intentionally twisted itself without trying into intricate hypnotic contact with the geometrically erotic entity that was invading her restless body, probing into her subtly throbbing asshole with new primalness, a bottomless love.

Touching

It is hard to understand how things touch, not because touching is difficult or somehow mysterious, not because of some insuperable occasionalism that governs it, but because touching itself takes place through hardness, the hardness it takes for anything to touch. But this happening-through-hardness also means that touching, even of the hardest blow, is deeply and truly soft, that touching is an arrival or event of what passes through or takes place within the in-and-out of hardness per se. (Whence the essentially transitional nature of erotic tactility, its being all about the becoming-hard of the soft and the becoming-soft of the hard. The softest lips are hard. The hardest cock is soft.) When it comes to touching, the best understanding can do is make contact with the cool fact of touching itself: things touch, how could they not?

Harder still to understand how Gemma touched the thing inside her with the intoxicating searchlight of her auto-reflective gaze—a profoundly and literally theoretical seeing-touching that was both discretely divided across and holistically all at once physical, imaginative, and intellective. Seamlessly nesting each aspect inside the other according to the inalienable hierarchy of her natural being, this triplex touching necessarily touched the thing by recursively touching itself along its own prismatic spectrum. In other words, the horny, soft-hard entry of the object into her loosening-tightening asshole set up tactile reverberations along the three-way insertion that Gemma herself always already is. And that is the strange gravitational truth about sticking it in, that the insertion touches the way one is here 'in the first place': body inside energy inside mind inside . . . ? The fatality of anal intrusion is that, far from establishing a magnetic relation to a known other, it opens an obscurer relation to an unknown, establishing an occluded *magmic* flow between external matter and the self-substance that mind is rooted within. Ass love probes through its very difference the dark boundary of the impersonal soul, touching it without contact, tapping a hole into which the invisible, like some sweet poisonous alien sap, flows. Ergo the paradoxical erotic aspiration to temporary permanency for the butt plug: not at all a closure, but a thing effecting sexual open submission to something intimately beyond oneself.

Concentrating on the unmistakable yet nonspecifiable feeling of her pink anus lustfully dilating around the gentle pressure of the strange form being subtly pulled upward under the taut, innocent hunger of her increasingly insatiable tender virgin ass, Gemma effortlessly touched it with every fiber, with all sensitive and intelligent tentacles of her being. Physically, she was confusedly suffused with the strangely indeterminate but centered sensation of her body embracing itself around the unfeelable tip of the self-buried thing, as if all nerves were seduced away from their stations to attend to its throbbing presence. Every cell, every muscle, all bodies within her body, each passively and inwardly supplicated itself, stretching langorously toward the slowly burning lower chamber, the ardent secret place where the de facto phallus uncannily communed with the innermost syrupy folds of her rosaceous anal core. The mysterious marriage happening there—a prismatic multiplication of the intensely specific sensation of the precious stretching of her probed ass ring and the indefinable rectal fullness pressuring her whole pussy into a moist aching mound of swollen flesh-petals—spread through her body, refracting its effects according to the differential capacities of its zones and members to receive them. It was in this receiving, in wholly opening her flesh from within to totally feel its being entered, that Gemma *saw* the object with a complete corporeal reflection of her own beauty, hypnotically grasping and shaping the inanimate thing to which she submitted into a slavish, hyper-submissive tool of hopeless lust. (The entity that made it stirred in his aeonic sleep.) Her tactile seeing, summoned from and through the entire overwhelming bodily spectacle of her sexual beauty, more specifically, its crisscrossing the lithe radiance of her pale limbs along the plane of their becoming increasingly saturated with the perversely irresistible plenitude of a young woman playing libidinously with her own butthole (overcoming lewdness via lewdness itself) . . . her seeing *projected* into the pleasurable object, entering the thing that was entering her, and thence reflected back ever more deeply from the object into all that was so openly touching it. Like a rainbow the tactile vision spread, starting/ending neither here nor there, but radiating without center into a pure, auto-sublimating kaleidoscope. It almost seemed like a half-ethereal snake with eyes for scales was passing in firm love-coils through her body. Eventually, soon, the serpent would find a way out and then Gemma, all that she ever was, would become nothing less than its new skin.

The formal content of this hypnotizing self-look, her haptic anal autogaze, consisted of an unnamable union of the three kinds of vision Gemma's whole being was hotly pushing and pressing into the ontic core of the object which she had lustfully shoved into her body less than an hour before.

Beyond representation, this look was yet secondarily legible on her face, whose special appearance was its very shadow or intimate negative projection. Her voluptuous visage, subtly but unmistakably flashing with patterns tied to the intertwining filaments of her inner gaze, generously gave off or spoke wondrously of the self-enveloping erotic gaze consuming her from within. Gemma's mouth, half opened and showing off her perfectly gapped and slightly crooked teeth whitely glowing above a glistening red tongue, gaped in infantile mimicry of how hungrily she was genitally fondling the ovoid form with hidden folds of her vibrant flesh. The aspirational sound coming from her elliptically open lips like a slowly exploding kiss figurally fulfilled the self-pleasuring sense of her total aesthetic or perceptual grasp of the self-ravishing possessing in full the whole complex of her pelvic cavity, speaking merely by its escape endless covert suggestions of an eventually over-whelming lust-pressure hotly increasing the tension of the invisible golden chain linking the hooded floral punctum of her ripe clit with the occult

depth of her succulent asshole. The
rising-falling pace of her breath com-
municated the expanding dilution of
tender-firm sensations spreading in
emanating waves across her whole
body and fitfully accentuating unpredictable points of her limber frame with
uncannily deep correspondences to the
core feeling of being entered from
behind. Like a secondary wave upon
this wave, the febrile dilation of her
nostrils exuded the phantasmagoric
power of her discriminatory imagination and self-seductive narrativization
of shameless masturbatory play, sug-
gesting a dangerous and titillating
abandonment of distinction between
inside and outside, an unfinishing
flirtation with losing the divide between fantasy and reality. The moisture
swirling through her sinus incrementally intimated with each breath
something of the fragrance being gener-
ated in the mimetic chamber of her
dreamy, aphrodisiac decay, its movement subtly displaying the innocent
olfactory intensity of her inner sensory
search for imminent orgasm. Gemma's
nose, saturated with the sweetening
smell of her own body, perfumely

glowed with the scent of her self-seduction, hinting at all the flowers to be found along the twisted imaginal path of auto-affective lust. Losing herself there, within the winding mnemonic movement of gazing into the feeling of her own projective sensory reflection, her eyes emitted the third and most powerful wave of the intoxicated hypnotic look. Slightly lowered, glassily moist, the green-hued spherules shone with the pure penetrating idea of her being penetrated, fully radiated the feeling of being filled. *Open me—I am open . . . I am open— open me.* Deliriously clear, they spoke in one second a trillion suggestions begging all at once, in the silent language of their inviolable clarity, for every lascivious violation, for the easy total enactment of every desire. Trapped within this triune light, the weird little toy now lay totally helpless, buried forever in the nothingness of being the pure tool, the zero term of such a beautiful one's absolute self-desire.

A skeptical reader, religiously bound to endless dualisms, may here wonder how a material object can be 'hypnotized' or how an ad hoc butt plug might so marvelously reflect the auto-erotic gaze of a girl. What about the object 'itself'? Answer: that is precisely what was never quite there. Nevertheless, something did happen to it. What begs to be figured out is how happening at once inhabits and transcends the distinction between *it* and *itself*, and correlatively, how an event may essentially affect a thing, indeed alter it to its very core, without concerning or even causally requiring there to be an in-itself at all. And that in fact is exactly what touching is, the dilatory event or expanding arrival of what always and only is between a thing and itself. That things touch, the being of touching, is the *manifest elision* of the existence of the in-itself, an ever proliferating and constantly mutating heresy against any and every definitional installation of the real. Touching is an untouchable ontic avant garde, an ungraspably perverse movement among things that never ceases showing them as they really are, namely, that they *never* really are. All touching is thus in some measure a hypnosis, the impinging of a thing towards stupefying suspension before its own nothingness, an external pressure pushing something towards abyssic self-intimacy. Of course tactual hypnosis is no kind of superadded effect or state, not a surface effect. It is simply and exactly the negative or subtractive intensification of the 'normal' hypnosis that constitutes anything's being itself (me-being), the non-stop helpless self-touching that every entity 'is'. So total touching wholly exposes things to their own emptiness (on both ends of the tactile spectrum: toucher & touched) such that whatever they are becomes inherently unhinged towards its own black hole or invisible void, leaving them bound to the weird freedom of being incapable of doing anything (and infinitely capable of doing nothing) on their own. Such a wholly touched thing persists in the paradoxical negative spontaneity of ungrounded dirigible contingency. It endures through a pure, zero-force determination or post-volitional intention to do what is willed of it, not to perform, but to immediately embody or incarnate the movement of its being touched, inside-outly *ad libitum* as it were. For the thing generously embedding itself into Gemma's bottom (which was precisely made, like other objects of fantastical repute, to actually be what one wants it to by means of refracting its reflection of what is projected into it back onto itself from within, like a mirror seeing itself with the gaze of its beholder), this meant becoming less and less a thing and more and more an expanding convolution of Gemma herself. Looking at it with the total feeling of her self-enchantment (a feeling that the object itself gravitationally co-implanted in Gemma through the secret field of its own perversely divine openness before such looking), Gemma's haptic gaze hypnotized the unfathomably pulsing anal form into becoming, via its inversely productive dissipation, more her than any part of her was. As she wanted it in her ass not as anything in particular, but solely as the site of her bottomless self-desire, so the thing did not become nor was experienced as any thing, but instead *melted* towards and into her body's own multiform auto-erotic intensification, its meta-haptic masturbation. She touched the small thing-that-should-not-be the one way it should be touched, the way it wanted to be touched. And it responded the only way it could, by letting itself expand around the center of its own strange indeterminacy into endless waves of all that Gemma desired (it) to be.

Feeling it so perfectly, Gemma was now irreversibly fitted to whatever was inside her perverted wet pink hole, hopelessly knotted to herself through the endlessly lustful opening it created and thus bound into a beautiful one-way union from which she would never, and never wish to, recover.

For less than a minute, the enticingly terrifying fact of this absolutely asymmetrical self-marriage clamped her psyche into a kind of temporary paralysis. Hypnotizer and hypnotized anarchically interchanged roles. Gemma's mind *froze* in infernal bliss before the twisted fate of being forever her own secret auto-whore.

Lost

The objectless look of concern starting
to overcome Gemma's expression spoke
perfectly of her predicament. The more
she *saw* her beauty into the thing
dilating her bottom, the more the thing
itself disappeared into being whatever
she wanted it to be—with emphasis on
whatever, in order to register the infinite multiplication of real fantasy the
experience was initiating her into.
Holding onto her own self via the
rosaceous velvet hole's tender ring,
Gemma was caught and enslaved
inside the deep open-endedness of
wanting. Rather than fulfilling her
fantasy, in the sense of actualizing a
lusted-for form, the thing embedded
and burrowed further and further into
the being of her desire, maximizing the
developmental scope of her lust in
tandem with the accelerating asymptot-
ic minimization of the thing itself.
Corporeally caught and psychically

stretched taught between a) an imagination sensuously flooded and saturated with uncountable pornographic forms, b) an intellect intensely focused on the intoxicating idea of being sodomized by her own beauty, and c) a sensorium totally fractured across the contradiction between the need for self-touching and the necessity of not doing so in order to preserve the ever-increasing pleasure, Gemma was lost.

The only way forward, the only way to find herself without destroying the experience that was irreversibly becoming her self, was *to do nothing*. But since doing nothing is impossible (given the seemingly inexorable progress of space-time, the fact of being, and so forth), Gemma instinctively fell into a way of doing it, of consciously holding acting at bay, which corresponded exactly to what one does when being lost. She nearly stopped moving and newly observed her surroundings. To do otherwise, above all, to do the one thing that was the hardest thing in the world not to do—finger her pussy—would be suicide. To survive, to preserve her own future tense against the excitement of the increasingly irresistible tension saturating and extending every networked node of her being, required letting all that is going to happen (to her) really happen, without interference. It meant *not* making or doing anything about it, precisely so nothing less than everything can and will happen. Otherwise there would be nothing, or possibly something even worse, merely more life, another day. To give in to the excitement, to simply fall into the thrill, would be to be lose the more tremendous fun of the thrill's own truth.

Doing nothing, letting everything happen (to her), all things come into view. What a relief. An incredible relief to feel and know that with every instant of staying lost she was coming closer to where she really was, each moment closer to coming than ever seemed possible. The room was now very dark, the sun gone behind the horizon, and the house only a rich ghostly veil covering from the eyes of no one the dangerous glow of her pleasure. Entering the narrow townhouse from the west side, you would walk two flights of stairs to find Gemma facing away from you in the back room she uses as a study. Still facing the window, she is sitting on a dark colored carpet with the couch behind her, hands holding shoulders above her knees and breathing easily down into her soft tummy, back slightly arched and catching most of her shadowy hair. With no clothing on now except the translucent blue panties pushed strangely around half of her bottom, the descending coolness of the air feels perfect on her pale flush skin, whose illusory blueness in the dark glows seductively with pink hues. Slowly examining her surroundings, letting her mind drift in the total bewilderment of it, everything swirling about Gemma was revealed as simultaneously alien, worthless, and beautiful. Nothing was cause for concern, but like the haphazardly grotesque and whimsical shapes her tossed clothing made here and there, everything was potentially interesting and even enchanting if given the proper attention. She looked down and saw her titties ripely suspended there, then slowly blinked her eyes with the thought of them being pulled, sucked. The near darkness of the outside was lovely, like a fluid dream in which thought could suddenly freely swim the whole world. How delightful it would be to stay here for the whole evening, fucked achingly slowly forever from behind by some gorgeous demon that would fly away if even once she turned round to glance at him. Or far better, to ravish herself until morning with nothing other than the permuting, pulsing thought of her own ravishment, so waywardly explore her own lush interior until . . .

Like a pool swimming with always more possibilities, doing nothing indoctrinated Gemma, soaked her ever deeper into the idea of anarchy, the endless domain of what is without beginning. Soul fed mind from this deep reservoir with an unstoppable invisible stream, which in turn became limitless expanding spheres of thought. The thought-spheres refractively projected illimitable prismatic images from all directions into her imagination, images her heart tirelessly distilled into licorous milky drops that were imbibed by every cell of her clean body. The self-penetrating pneumophantasmological cascade of meta-sexual soul-dew was overwhelming. And the flow,

however slowed by the universal
waterfall of ontic translation, was still
too much. To save herself from explo-
sive drowning she had to *focus*, that is,
resort to a fairly fraudulent way of
doing nothing that serves when no
other option is possible. Unknowingly
inspired by the very structure of her
own being's descending distillation, a
pouring-into-itself that fused with and
proportionally fulfilled the form of her
internal dilation, Gemma focused then
on the feeling of sucking that caught
her fantasy a moment ago when she
glanced down at her tits. *The world will
milk me . . . a thing beyond the world
will milk me through it. World-as-mouth
will lick and suck into the beyond this
liquid perversion welling up inside me.*
Yet resisting the need to focus as far as
possible, she also refused to imagine
anything in particular about this object
of focus, but held firm at the pure
thought of her breasts being sucked,
forcing the whole present order of
being as it were into the indiscrete
position of being nothing but whatever
is doing the sucking. She became
consumed with the thought of being
nourishingly consumed (a consumption

that only nourishes the consumed itself) and now really started to *give in* to what was going to happen through this simple gift, the absolute letting-be-tasted of her pointed mounds of super-fluous carnal succulence. Realizing this potentiality in truly anarchic terms, as a gift that gives itself to itself without remainder, Gemma effectively instruct-ed her own living breast flesh, taught and drew it out into the fact of its being orally fondled using nothing other than its own capacity to be so—revealing the secret link between breasts and peda-gogy that makes smart horny schoolgirls smile.

Pushing themselves into the pure feeling, Gemma's nipples swelled and slightly protruded into their own vacu-umous dilation, inversely demonstrating themselves eager to become firm instruments of oral pene-tration—a feeling like a tonguing mouth teasing out her breast-openings, conjuring a way of teasingly engorging them into opening like tight flowers. Rosebuds her nipples would become, mysteriously oozing with Marian, virginal milk-semen in an obscenely floral swollen protrusion rendering them profanely capable of being shallowly probed. As if the areolae of her extrasensitive shade or astral body were indeed erecting into tiny strawberry penises whose soft tips were in turn wetly sucking into themselves the penetrating tongues licking them into form. Intoxicated with the feeling of such double nested interpenetration, Gemma had to bridle her imagination, bind her fantasy to itself within the simple domain of self-feeling in order to endure it, to avoid in one breath being swept away. Responding perfectly to this restriction, her throbbing anus, orally activated by Gemma's firm holding at bay of the thought of lustful mouths playing torturously with her horny nipples, sucked itself around the ovoid form intruding the interior of her rear. The perversely auto-intimate sensation of this sublimely anal backwards hunger instinctively opened Gemma's mouth further around the dreamy feeling of a voidal phallus feeding itself past her lips. Viscous saliva saturated her linguistic love-hole and oozed limpidly from the tingly souring orifice to fall like pre-cum on her pinkly flushed bosom and inwardly back into her steamy throat, as if in longing to lube herself all the way down from within. The soft core of the resonating anal-oral link tightened pleasurably through the clitoral knot of her now spongy cunt, causing Gemma to gently flex her abdomen and inch the curvature of her corporeal lust incrementally toward the ouroboric. Mouth, pussy, and ass now invisibly extended into each other's domains across a dangerous three-way field of feeling that itself wanted, gravitationally, to expand into an outrageous orgiastic scene of phantasmagoric, even hermaphroditic masturbation, onanism of a sublimely beautiful and monstrous order that would require no activity or devices other than the endlessly swelling vibration of its own pleasure. Gemma looked down, sighing hotly towards the puffy sweet folds of her tempting mound, inwardly gazing all her loveliness into the thing that was arousing her so ideally from within, thinking in perfect self-command: *fuck me*.

With her desire held firmly but without tension inside the triune being-perverted process of her mouth-pussy-

ass relation, Gemma had to work harder, which necessarily also meant more
easily, at not doing anything. It was
hard to allow thought to enter her
without touching it, without fondling
its heady forms into the thrill of excited
effects. All the more so—and this is the
essential bind of consciousness—when
each thought, in being allowed to pass
unattended, only opened space for a
more enticing, potentially more pressing thought still. The promise of
fantasy is not realized by entertaining
it, but by en*during* it, letting yourself be
opened by its hardness until the hardness itself becomes perfectly,
superiorly soft. Imagine all that Gemma
had to endure along this three-fold axis,
this *tre-palium* of blissful auto-erotic
torment whereon desire-thought itself,
like a degenerate runaway slave, was
racked and punished. First came the
half-notion of how nice it would be to
be able to lick her own pussy, especial-
ly while deeply fingering her asshole
until surprising girl-cum squirts all
over tummy, face, and tits. What
shameful yummy fun self-cunnilingus
might be, contortionally disappearing
oneself into a kind of autophagous

fleshly pastry. Followed by the thought that not being able to is even better, more pleasurable to ache and moan and spit across forbidden distance, doubling the relation into a mutual arc or bow of ecstasy in which mouth pussied and pussy mouthed until both came impossibly together in an iterated shock twistingly traversing the electric line from crown to anus. Then came the more mundane thought of sitting rearly stuffed on a throbbing phallus while a secret girlfriend lavished oral love all over and around her swollen clit, the countless cumming turning Gemma's limbs to electric jelly and earning the girl's slavish lips deep pussy-tasting kisses plus all the thick semen the stud pulls out to fountain towards their panting mouths. Followed by sixty-nining with someone who ties her up, ankles roped down to thighs, hands bound together behind, being inescapably devoured as the pulsing of her nether ring around a bulbous glass plug never ceases pushing everything squirmily over the edge of constrained abandon.

Then a better more endless thought: being skewered on a self-penetrating spiral phallus that enroots itself impossibly out of her engorged clit. Erecting at a surprising yet torturously pleasant pace, like a shedding snake the fresh pink penis vines willfully and blindly across her white tummy, oozing dewy fluid as it glides between breasts to finally enter a heady orifice that by now self-incestuously pants for its syrupy fullness. Leaving barely less than enough time to finish playfully tonguing its still-developing strawberry head, the female cock stiffens sufficiently to begin fuckgrowing into Gemma's softly gagging and almost orgasming mouth. In a sublime duration of oral onanistic ravishment, it pushes too far, curving down into her gullet, somehow preventing spasm and indeed aiding soft breath by its own firm presence, strangely sensitizing all it touches with the circuit of its own feeling skin. Seeking entry via Gemma's insides to its own sub-phallic interior, the tentacular growth travels downwards like a parallel spine of flesh, burning with the sense of its continuous expansion from pussy mound to hyper-clitoral tip. The swelling self-invader, excited by its wayward probing, descends through Gemma's lithe and lightly twisting torso into her lower belly along an impossibly direct course. Soon it is filling her nervous rectum like a loving, self-purifying tumescent worm, a carnal, semi-animal enema from an immanent beyond. Her whole frame sweatily pulsing in queasy lust for the impending reemergence, Gemma begins to fondle the outside of her ripe anal ring, maieutically teasing the compressing cock-head towards birth as it mushrooms outward, oozing creamy emissions. At last it pushes fully past the rudely protruding rose-bud, which relaxes into tightening around the semi-flexible rod as she tenderly strokes and squeezes the self-lubricated shaft closer and closer to squirting. Unable to any longer resist the transcendent sensory perfection of this priapic desecration, and needing to ensure its continuance along a proper path, Gemma now stimulates with her whole left hand the cock thrusting out of her ass as she squeezes the obscene vine at its Venusian base with her right. Stiffening within the double manipula-tion, it requires more and firmer touching to be guided circumferentially around into the creamy folds of her fertile pussy, until all of a sudden the intensifying circuit of titillating enforcement makes the whole contorted torsal loop flex in intense impaling orgasm, clamping Gemma's mouth towards her drool-covered chest and enflaming her whole belly as the extravagant organ spouts androgynous cum, saturating and entering her entire vagina in one thrusting moment. Positionally crippled by her own uncontrollable lust, Gemma stays this way for a good few minutes: groping and stroking and throatily sucking the thickly softening phallus which bridges her pussy and mouth, spasming in a torturous sprial of nested penetration, squeezing the self-entwining prick between her breasts and pushing it further out her ass as she lets her infinitely beautiful cunt be fucked by nothing less than her own oral sodomy.

Supremely lost in a zone of almost paralyzed indistinction between thought and reality, Gemma ardently conceived and witnessed these and similar ideas, desperately doing nothing other than doing nothing. Now she was at her limit, at the threshold where passivity cannot but twist itself into extreme passion. Heroically she held her three-fold being (mind, energy, body) on this threshold in complete prurient correlation to her three lust-filled openings (mouth, pussy, ass). Mouth openly dripped with the idea of being penetrated by her own beauty, saturating her wet-pantied pussy in an endless swirl of swelling erotic forms, each of which in turn took slow pleasure in filling her insatiable wanton ass with deeper ideas of her own loveliness. The asymptotically intensifying auto-erotic loop—closer and closer to but never cumming—was unbearable, less and less but always barely endurable by virtue of its own continuous flow. She could and could not stay this way forever. It was dark. She wanted to move, to give expression to the movement coiling her infinite soul into an interminable spiral of self-love. Yet she kept herself there, owning herself in total erotic self-possession, drinking fully the intoxication of being so perfectly in-between, bonding herself to sexual self-enslavement with her own unfinishing fondling of the curvy orgasmic limen. If anything pushes her over to the other side, it will be something *other than herself*. So completely did Gemma recursively distill each drop of desire into her body, so alchemically transmute the entire expanding secret archive of inner porn into her very flesh—*ars totam requirit feminam*—that there is no one who can find her. A secret treasure, even to her herself, Gemma floated far away and here, ecstatically gazing with desire upon all sides of her perversely divine body, floating in a night lit only by the luminous hue of its own pleasure. Only a god can save her.

Me

Three protracted spasms, all centered on the thing within her that was not her, slowly shook Gemma's body. The first drew in the exposed end of the object, enveloping it fully inside her anus in a single, slow, quivering throb. The second electrically sucked the arcane form all the way within the red inebriated depth of her lily-white bottom. The third pulsed everywhere at once around the dark thing in a singular unthinkable pelvic kiss which radiated in waves like a golden floral tremor out into her fingers and toes. Two facts now fused into a single undisputable truth: 1) the ovoid thing was no longer inside her body; 2) something new was in the room. The non-duality of these facts was such that they must be seen non-dialectically. It is not that the object disappeared materially and reemerged in another form. Nor is it that something entered the room which displaced the object. All that happened happened perfectly the way it did, independently of any hidden ground or occult causality. The appearance and the disappearance were a unitary, simple event, neither definable nor indefinable in terms of either aspect. Likewise, the new being in the room with Gemma was neither her nor someone else, but an absolutely recognizable divinely radical novelty whose existence was infinitely alien and natural. Put simply, it was the apotheosis of her own presence.

At home on this new remote plateau, Gemma finally knew there was never anything to lose. It did not matter whatsoever that anything was happening—specifically, that her body was subtly locked in weirdly slow throes of an endless almost-orgasm, that her imagination was impossibly saturated with an infinite array of sublime perversions, and that her intellect had fashioned itself into a mystically profane mirror, an absolutely sexy autospeculum projecting the totality of her irresistible beauty into every dilating pore of her being. All of a sudden—and without any transformation at all—it was at last the easiest thing in the universe to let everything happen, to delight in the never-ending domain of being nothing other herself, whatever that was. A perfectly wayward and wandering path now lay clear and open before her, the way into a uniquely limitless and new life. All that was required was to immolate herself on the hyper-private altar of auto-love, to perish erotically by means of the imperishable onanistic intoxication of being *me*. Perhaps it did not matter how she did it, this way or that, upside down or right side up. However she passes the portal into earthly paradise she will have passed it. And yet precisely because the style of her passing to the immanent beyond was arbitrary, because she was the absolutely free priestess of her own abysmal self-initiation, she wanted it to be perfect, that is, supremely all at once playful, simple, and perverse.

Gemma stood up slowly and went to the window, where the glass was quickly cooling in the sunless autumn air. The warm rush of blood through her loosened knees made the movement feel like floating. Now she turns on the lights on either side of the wide sill, letting the glow summon the ghostly image of her bare body in the evening before her, frozenly hovering in the darkening atmosphere. Never did her pale flesh appear more unreal. Not because of the spectral effect, or because she was something essentially other than it, but because the image paradoxically revealed itself to be so insuperably *more* real than the body it reflected. So intensely and superiorly real was the very reflection that the reality of the flesh it showed was fatally suspended, afloat in a void of unknowable night. Being irrevocably possessed by her own corporeal beauty, Gemma clearly saw—actually and not in imagination—that her image, in its inherent infinity, was totally more real than her. So that her body seemed substantially more liquid than solid, its liquidity more gaseous than liquid, and its gaseousness more insubstantial than gas. Being herself a speculative reality, she seemed more in the mirror than anywhere else, forever alive in the crystal purity of its perfect oblivion. Now that she no longer needed a mirror to see herself, the mirror became an insanely enchanting portal, a space that, far from doubling the given, rendered openly visible the limitless domain where it never was. Ecstasy.

Staring into the deep plutonic distance of her non-reflecting pupils, Gemma peripherally saw herself push down her panties, let them fall to her feet, and step out of them in pure nakedness nearer to the window. She watched herself watch herself, lost in her own eyes, turning her waist to feel the impossible curvature of the imminent, inconceivable pleasure which the becoming-genital of her whole body will provide. Womanly she played with her image in the glass for a little while, caressing her curved lines with semitrembling fingers and letting the focus of her internal eye stroke the whole length of ever-expanding lust as it gently dilated more and more the wanton core of her tight body becoming secretly split open from dark mystic crown to barely gaping rosebud. Until it was time to turn round, arch her back, and with a long over-the-shoulder rearward gaze, take in the full splendor of her ripening ass. Showing off to nothing, she parted her pale cheeks, glimpsed the shadowed glow of the pink anal ring-petal nestled in the downy cleft. Below she ocularly made out—deeply kissed with both eyes—the inverted swollen mound of her pussy, its moist parted symmetry, and perceived the inexplicable sense with which it begged to be desperately proximate to the sweet sodomy of perfect self-penetration.

How to plumb what happens to pussy when 'its' ass is amorously opened? Pussy does not possess ass properly speaking, but it does preside over ass in a perversely complicit way, so that what ass undergoes can totally concern it. And when it is deeply and unavoidably concerned, pussy is fully possessed by ass without displacement, in a manner that reciprocally makes ass wholly pussy's. When pussy is thus perfectly usurped by ass, it paradoxically comes both into full possession of ass and into an overwhelming self-fulfillment that is otherwise unattainable, that is, as long as it is in the service of itself. The posterior ecstatically unlocks the superior, opening from behind the expanse of its beyond. So that the ass, proportionally liberated from being itself, also as it were exults in saying to pussy, *I am wholly yours*. It is from the lush position of this possession that *my ass* are terribly intoxicating words for a beautiful woman to speak, words that make her whole body intemperately swell and melt into pussy, genitively unlacing her into being its slavish possession. Absent the anal element, pussy is hers. But in the presence of it, she is *its*, a slave of its endless inverse enslavement to ass. Losing her pussy to her ass, it comes back to her a thousand-fold in the form of her own utter abandonment to the infinite recursion of her pussy (pussy of pussy of pussy . . .) around the total groundlessness of anal lust, the satisfying insatiability or full zero of wanton ass( )hole.

Speculating inside the intoxicating abyss of her own rear beauty, Gemma subtly swayed and lost herself in the feeling of her behind, in the impossibly pleasurable fact of being wholly *before* what she was within. *That is me—what am I?* Now she felt the terrifying exteriority of her own desire. That irresistible angel floating effortlessly in the void before her, who was far more herself than she—like a disoriented entity she longed to see *her*, that gorgeous horny girl-species, ravished in the ass, a *her* that was both her own body and something more: the actual living form of her own being, the ultimate analogon whose breath is one's own. Now, through *it*, she would finally enter herself. By letting it enter her.

Looking with all beauty both inwardly and outwardly at the virginally open asshole of which her whole body was simply the golden baroque frame, Gemma's consciousness pierced itself at the point where her left middle finger now entered its moistness, losing the haptic tip of her exteriority in the pink, tickly vestibule. Utterly freely she fingered herself reversely in front of the dark window, neither with timidness nor abandon. With the gentleness of a growing plant she frictioned the slick puckered hole into waves of novel delight, summoning secret milk within the folds below. So gently, without hurry . . . yet all of a sudden she is cumming powerfully, totally unable to distinguish between the parts of her that are and those that are not. A gift of nothing that turns out to be everything—"the passage from the inside out, from the outside in, the passage between us, is limitless. Without end. No knot or loop, no mouth ever stops our exchanges" (Irigaray). This was beyond fingering herself; it was penetrating her penetration by a single tendril of the hyper-iconic image. Whatever happened that so little could push her so far? Pure meta-embarrassing perfect equation of groundlessness and everything getting wet. Abandonment to the peace and gentleness of peasantly simple, unassuming ravishment. Limply with a smile, the *mirror in the girl* fell off a marine cliff and plunged to her death.

Gemma, impossibly still and more present, turned around and fell back like a love-struck subject onto the couch behind her, giving the sound of her breath to the world in generous, sincerely overplayed waves. Dark hair fell chaotically and clung like sighing tentacles upon her sweaty breasts. Quivering belly rose and fell past her hip bones. And she stared down her image—supine with head up and feet bent down to the floor—as if it were her enemy. *I am going to make you*

*squeal and squirm, watch you hold onto
yourself for sweet life as I curve through
a passage you didn't know you had.*
Vengefully fixed on herself, Gemma
raised her knees back toward her
shoulders, exposing the pristine folds
of her pussy to the night's openness,
laying open her posterior funnel to
further play. The juice which had
pooled around her clit now drooled
back down, waiting to be mixed with
saliva into a syrupy lube. Maintaining
her self-gaze with unbelievable seri-
ousness, Gemma tongued with taunting
slowness the middle two fingers of her
right hand, coating them for intimate
insertion before sliding the twinned
digits down to the delicately wrinkled,
elastic orifice. Stacking the finger tips
pad to nail, Gemma sunk them in
halfway with one motion, cradling the
swollen underside of her bewildered
vagina. Now laying open the palm of
her hand to fully show the angle of
entry, she panted there like a tired
panther, gloating almost lazily over the
to-be-devoured life of her beauty, her
prey. Right forearm tucked under right
hip—left forearm holding down and
back her left thigh. Pursing her asym-

metrically open lips, she pulled the
fingers all the way in, exposing the
strong curve of her bicep and making
taught the abdomen ridge of down to
her mound. With head and hips cocked
contortionally towards each other,
Gemma loves watching the girl helplessly feel the fingers twitch and twist
inside the deep shallow of her velvety
anus, teasing her g-spot into spongy
firmness. She gloats over what she is
about to do her, sighs debauchedly, and
then started to plunge and pull her
pulsing fingers strongly inside, careful-
ly observing each desirous distortion of
the expectant face. Probing herself with
the alimentary persistence of a worm,
she sees the girl's tongue semi-
consciously creep outward in propor-
tion as her glistening cunt steadily
swells and splays open from the hungry
interior pressure. Compressed little
breaths start pushing up from her
abdomen and whimpering in spurts,
inhaled and exhaled across her re-
strained voice. Gemma knows she has
her when she feels her two fingers,
slick on the perineum in a subtle
creamy froth, being pushed gently
outward by the mushy inner ring of her

exquisitely abject flesh-rose. Digging the tips of her free hand into her left ass check, Gemma smiles to see the girl writhe around her taught, involuntarily tensing core. She relaxes the phallic digits for a little while, allowing the helplessly distracted-concentrated nymph some arrhythmic moments to circulate a few more drops of love-milk into her secretly engorged cum-gland. Then moves firmly to make her orgasm, soaking in the white-hot image of her quivering erect titties, the high-pitched breath, her curling toes . . . only now *she* is wholly trapped lewdly open and suddenly squirting like a dying *jet d'eau* all over herself, lapping with disoriented lust at the clear sweet water as it hits Gemma's chest and wets the pale insides of her tingling thighs.

A little longer Gemma lay there, rocking her head in strange delightful dismay—the incredibly happy sinking in of the fatal fact that she was irreparably on her way to being really gone, no longer ever in need of looking forward to anything. A whim of her left index finger traced *Gemma* on her moist tummy, permuted the letters to senselessness. She thought of the object

something possessed her to slip into
her bottom—no longer there, yet not
gone. Rather all the more present in an
unpredictable way, like Beatrice to
Dante when he lost the way and followed his prick in the name of pity. It
is weird when something dies inside of
you and makes you more alive, espe-
cially when it opens being a total self-
slut as the only, inescapable way to
paradise. Everything atmospherically
showed itself to be more watery than
water, a hyper-marine element next to
which water is dust. A kind of auto-
naiad signaled Gemma up from the
couch, gave her specific instructions to
crouch on all fours, arch her back, and
not to look around. Which she did, and
immediately looked back into the
window-mirror of the night—to feel a
stinging slap of the reflection-mistress
spanking herself upon Gemma's bottom, rosying her white lobes with
warmth. *I want whatever you will do to
me.* Gemma dropped and turned her
head to the floor, twisting to free her
left arm. From this low position she
could no longer observe her image in
the window, but mobile imagination
saw everything precisely as it was—a

perverted young girl on the upstairs floor of her house raising three saliva-laden fingers from her mouth to her butt. Coinciding with the insertion of the soft triune tips, the auto-domina initiated an arousing-humiliating inner dialogue that exercised a kind of liturgical power over Gemma's experience. *Do you . . . Tell me . . . I am . . . Please . . . Say it . . . Yes.* The unvoiced verbal exchange talked herself into a new depth of erotic abasement, like a sinful confessional sinking both priest and sinner into some long lost Elysium. Without restraint, she felt herself bound there, privately examined, captivated by the power of her own submission. The fingers softly pried open the pink, flaring opening of her fully relaxed bunghole, sinking into her slowly like something falling to an ocean floor. Abandoned, derelict in the darkening abyss of unfathomable desire, Gemma's soul bobbed and swam and sank ever deeper into the helpless delirium of hopeless buggery. When at last the third orgasm began, it was torturously slow, wrapping her torso in deep breath-stealing spasms, like a pythonic cord spiraling around her veiny neck all the way down around her upturned hips, its firm tail pressuring gently hard against the aching clitoris. Finally the deep waves subsided and Gemma hung in heaven there, lightly convulsing all over as her electrified anus unclamped itself from cumming, kissing into herself the final shallow loving stabs of her lady's fingers. Now slumping to the floor, her eyelids wet with tears from the excessively blissful strain, Gemma returns the three fingers to her parted mouth, tongues and breathes upon their slick musky sweetness, hesitantly tastes the heady flower of her gaping tail, and for many minutes almost sleeps there, sucking like a dreaming baby on herself, a limp pale body all tingling and flush with secret terrible power.

Gemma's mind drifted from her corpus and flew like a lost bird toward the rising moon. Had she ever had a lover? She could not remember. The heart, memorial interface between soul and body, no longer held answers, for it was becoming all answer, answer itself, the omnipresent seat of happiness. The idea was to beat her wings higher and higher, pierce the bubble of the widest

sphere. Yet the further she ascended,
the more space curved around her so
that stars swam in the sea from which
she arose and the only way to the
summit lay in swooping down upon
her flesh, seizing it in the sharpness of
utopic lust-love. Like Zeus-becoming-
swan Gemma shot and fell headlong in
hot will to ravish the superior form of
her body. So fast that in one motion she
stood up and entered herself from
outside the window she faced herself
in, embracing the way Narcissus wanted to the secret rear side of her mirror
image. Left hand gripping hip and right
easing down the small of her back into
the begging-to-be-parted cheeks of her
rapt ass, she now coaxed four fingers
into the burning, luxurious hole. On
wobbly, barely bent knees she stood,
almost hanging from her hand as if it
were the conic terminus of some futur-
istic, decadent anal hook-stool. Let her
get used to it for a minute. Let her body
open to find a new way of enclosing
what it wants. Loving to see her species
so caught, Gemma soon jiggled and
pulled her fingers inside the girl so
firmly that she started at once to shake
and twist from the hot surprise. It was a

joy to see her legs tense and stretch in choreographic response to the intrusion, her abdomen flex and curl as if lifting her cunt in some ritual offering, her neck stiffening and relaxing while holding her head down upon the glowing skinscape, her wayward mouth, as if incapable of ceasing to whisper unspeakable desires to itself, sweetly drooling with pure animal desire over the plentiful milky surface of steaming me-lust. The feeling was hard to hold within a bipedal frame. Easing her to bend over and support herself left arm to knee, Gemma found further access to the pliant ass, easily sinking all four fingers in to the hilt. Crouching forward over herself, letting her hair fall to the floor, Gemma gave her prey into the loving probing, made her lose herself in being let loose upon the pleasurable almost-exiting of pleasure from my desire-bound body. *I want to flee, but the uncanny promise of my unknown lust insists on me (staying), makes me (do things), decides (me) to do nothing – I didn't know I could make me do this to myself for you.* The observation of the so-natural surrender made slick puffy pussy ache and swell, a soft internal tightening making everything so open that when the impossible impending contraction came, it was only a further opening, an expansion into the most novel and blissful ease. With rhythmic concentration Gemma libidinally *relaxed* herself into intensely limpid sexual self-intrusion, letting the girl-mirror fall to pieces all over into herself. Maybe it had nothing to do with sex, but was a perfectly simple passing beyond it, a perversion so natural that it instantly erased its own sexuality. The pleasure was totally libidinal—a gorgeous girl desperate with hardcore desire for nothing other than anally fucking itself to hot orgasm—but she was entirely somewhere else. No telling whether or how many times Gemma made Gemma cum like this. So saturated, so seamlessly stretched across the psychical rack of erotic self-love, her wayward soul, drunk on the hot wine of its possessor body, sank upright into the innate bliss of doing nothing, everything it wanted it to. Again Gemma came to herself, alive to the lovely alien music of her rising-falling breath, her intimately audible sodomitical sighs. Hair clung to her moist, flush face. She cupped and squeezed my breasts from behind, caressing Gemma's sides as the self-perfumed body slumped to the floor. Anally releasing from all need of ever knowing what to do with herself, she curled to a semifetal position, smiling in the subtle warmth blanketing those perfect thighs. Little hands secretly fondling insatiable folds. Rapt in the gravity of what is already happening next.

Summoned by the sheer power of her own becoming-open, Gemma stood upright before her image. From head to toes she felt queasy and courageous with fatal desire to offer herself in sacrifice to the infinity of her own carnal need—gazing beauty into the image's stare and staring into the beauty of the image's gaze. All the way. The radical fact *that* she was beautiful, the sheer self-evident thought of it, suffused Gemma's mind, making it flash uncontrollably in a kind of infinitely intelligent stupor of itself. The pure perceptual *what* of her beauty, the material constellation of all (and none) of the impossible-to-describe details of the luscious body that you are imagining for yourself, filled Gemma's eyes,

making each of her five senses synaes-
thetically pulse and glow with the
perfect lithe plentitude of naturally
intoxicating erotic charm. And the
flowing phantasmatic *how* of her beauty, a subtle energy-feeling or cordial
hinge holding thought and perception
inside a singular spectral haunting,
impregnated Gemma's imagination,
causing it to swarm spermatically with
innumerable visions and memories and
concepts of her unique, eternally
individuated hotness. All three levels
of vision triunely fused and twisted
through the overwhelmingly positive
negative identity of the inverted reflection. Finding the secret, mystical non-
duality of her hypnosis of the image
and the image's hypnosis of her, Gemma's consciousness swirled and
coalesced without diminishment
around the occult ground of her beauty's identity: the lovely darkness of her
self-dilated anus—the supreme nether-
pupil through which Gemma paradisi-
cally saw, felt, and thought herself.
Ringed with its own beautiful unique
kind of monocular pink lip, Gemma's
asshole, through the medium of her
expanded interior vision, kissed per-

fectly like a panting mouth the equally and all-the-more lovely gaping anal flower of the specular twin. A girl naturally in love with herself will sometimes kiss a mirror, finding a moment's pleasure in suppressing the material fact that the glass cannot give what she wants. Some fall into the deeper delight of touching themselves in front of a mirror, flirting as far as they can sustain it in the distant shallows of speculative onanism. Only Gemma, the princess-queen of spontaneous innocent sexual perversity, actually touched herself in the mirror the only way possible: moist rosy anus openly kissing itself around the secret revelation of perfect self-lust, in the occult inversely oral intimacy of its visible non-reflection. Unmentionable exemplar of all girl-girl kissing scenes.

Drinking her spirit in through this absolute portal of self-lust, Gemma's anus throbbed and swelled in desire of all she wanted to do, willfully pressuring her tight pussy into an extravagant pool of swollen wetness. Her inner anal flesh pillowly filled the space created by the sphincter-dilation, exposing new surface domains for lustful self-expansion. Desperate to totally fill herself with herself, Gemma felt her left hand reach back and sink the tip of its middle finger into the puffy, flush rosebud. Like some inverse anemone her tender butthole withdrew into its inner exterior, opening in fulfillment of its own needing to be stuffed. Right hand too reached back and caressed the sensitive warm slippery ring. Gaping paradoxically all the more under the lightest, tender touch, Gemma's divine under-oculus widened seamlessly with desire, invisibly releasing more and more beauty into the auto-erotic speculum-circuit, saturating the magical *tertium quid* of the mirroring itself with the supreme sodomitical magnetism of her self-capturing gaze. A picture of her at this moment would show a meta-photogenic, camera-melting girl symmetrically holding her pink asshole almost inordinately open as she panted for herself in the darkness of the window-mirror. Think all in Chloe des Lysses's look that Agamben's reading suppresses—the open blind spot of the philosopher's profaning, decisional gaze. But the reality was superior: Gemma's ass is dilating *her*. Freely

submerged inside the radically immanent vision-stance of infinite auto-
erotic gravity, the soul itself was being
sucked in always a little further, forever
in expanding advance of its own satura-
tion. *Pondus meum, amor meus.*

A newly tremendous and terribly
beautiful emotion—interrupting without intervention the feral intention to
fist herself silly—overcame Gemma,
caused her to spontaneously cum in
unceasing surpassing of her ability to
do so. All she could do was hang on,
with nothing left to hang on to. All she
did was barely something, simply see
her perfect nudity, for the first, paradi-
siacal time. You cannot look upon her.
It is impossible. (The impossibility of
looking upon her is you.) As her green
eyes welled with rare tears. As she saw
her wet mouth drool and kiss itself
with imperishable sweetness. As she
held herself for dear death before the
happy beauty of her body. As tears fell
down pink cheeks and wet her pulsing
neck. As saliva sank towards the fragrant feminine groin. As her hands, by
only holding themselves there, contin-
ued to fill the whole body with pure
potentialities of touch. As the tears

could not stop streaming and joined
themselves into tiny rivulets lacing her
torso. As her viscous saliva did the
same, rolling in rich globules inside
itself, reaching even the downy small of
her back. As she spread her ass cheeks
further in preparation to receive the
strange, necessary baptismal flow. As
the hot salt tears merged and intersect-
ed with her lascivious spittle,
slickening in front the puffy outer labia
and in back forming a single stream of
liquid *me* about to descend into the
steamy rear cleft. As she moaned and
twisted herself, turning for a moment
her head to spit and drip a spermy
excess of mouth juice straight down to
the middle of her upward arching
bottom. As hands softly spread her ass
cheeks a little further to show forth the
full abysmal glory of Gemma's perfectly
gaping open anal rose. As the swirling
drops of sweat and tears and saliva
descended her body in glistening
swarms, following the hyper-haptic
gravity of her orgasmic skin, its perversely self-consuming intelligence. As
the substantial infinity of her soul
squeezed and distilled itself into an
impossibly pleasurable flow, a liquid

procession of unquenchable auto-lust. As her insatiable and innocent asshole received and sucked in the liquid plenitude of all that was given to it, the nine liminal pink folds confirming like a fleshy heretical font the irreparability of the event. As Gemma exploded without fragmentation into uncountable erotic unities. As all dreams dissolve into coming true.

gnOme is a secret press. "Here, being neither oneself nor someone else" (Pseudo-Dionysius). It specializes in the publication of anonymous, pseudepigraphical, and apocryphal works from the past, present, and future. "Identity is the primal form of ideology." Send inquiries and submissions to gnOmebooks@gmail.com. "I am halfway between these appearances and *that* which invalidates them, *that* which has neither name nor content, *that* which is nothing and everything" (Michel). You never do anything anyway. "It is no longer I who live" (Saul).